Just Enough
Patience

This is a work of fiction. Any similarities to any real persons, living or deceased, are purely coincidental and not intended by the author.

ISBN : 978-1-7372941-3-9

Printed in the United States of America
First Edition June 2021

The Demetria Davis Foundation Inc.

For Elyse,
I dedicate this book to Elyse. Keep your burning desire for new knowledge and continue to go after everything you want in life. Your wittiness and energy is unmatched! Thank you for being you, because of you I am no longer anxious when I have to wait, I sit back and let the time pass because I know what is meant for me is on it's way.

I love you forever and always,
Mommy

"Just, Just, wake up! You've gotta get up.
It's an emergency!" shouted Joy.
"OMG, you sleep like a bear in hibernation!"

"This better be a real-life emergency,
or I'm gonna get you for interrupting
my beauty sleep!" I said.

"Looks like you're gonna need
a lot more beauty sleep," mumbled Joy.
"What?" I questioned as I rubbed my eyes.

"I said I have my first loose tooth; look at it.
It's literally hanging on by a thread,"
Joy said with her mouth wide open,
blowing her breath to make her tooth sway.

"And...why is this such big news?" I asked.
"Helloooo? Earth to Just.
Didn't you get a visit from the tooth fairy
when you lost a tooth?
If we get this thing out,
we'll have saved enough money
to go to the movies!" Joy reminded me.

This is my little sister, Joy.
Her hobbies include annoying me,
getting me in trouble,
and copying everything I do.
Still, I do have to admit she's pretty awesome.
She's super smart, obsessed with learning,
and very athletic.

"I've been researching all morning
how to get this tooth out quickly and painlessly.
I have a couple of theories for us to try.
Come on!" demanded Joy.

"Girls, what is going on in here?
What time is it?" Mom questioned.

"It wasn't me. Joy dragged me out of bed!
We all know how she can get
when she has her scientist coat on," I explained.

"Look, Mom, look at it! My tooth is even looser!"
Joy shouted with excitement.
"Honey, what did Mom say about the loose tooth?"

"You said to be patient—when the time is right,
it will come. But, Mom, I researched it
and there are ways to get your tooth out.
Do NOT worry, it is safe.
I repeat, do NOT worry," explained Joy.

"I know you're excited.
Losing your first tooth is a big deal!
But, sometimes, when we force things,
we end up hurting ourselves.
It's best to just be patient.
I'm going to try
to get a little more sleep," said Mom.

"Sleep tight, Mommy,"
said Joy with a sneaky look in her eyes.
"This isn't a good idea, Joy,"
I whispered to my little sister.
"Okay, got it!"

"Joy, what are you doing with the toaster?" I asked.

"So we're going to tie the string—
one end around my tooth
and one end around the toaster.
Then, I'll stand at the top of the stairs,
and we'll drop the toaster. Remember,
we CAN'T wake up Mom!
So, you're going to put a pillow in the spot
where the toaster will land. Got it? Great, let's go!"
Joy grabbed me by the arm and dragged me
to the staircase in a hurry.

"Are you ready?" Joy silently mouthed to me
as I was nervously standing next to the pillows.

"I really don't think this is a good idea,"
I whispered from below.

Joy reached over the railing and tossed the toaster.
Down went the toaster, the string, and...
"No tooth," I said.

"A scientist always tests different theories,
on to theory number two.
Let's go back into the kitchen,"
said Joy, rushing down the stairs.
She walked into the kitchen
and opened the refrigerator.

"Perfect, I'm starving.
What do we have in there for breakfast?"
I said with a sigh of relief.

"Here it is! This one will be easy—
I just have to bite into this apple,
and the firmness of it will grip my tooth.
When I move the apple away from my mouth, voilá!
My tooth will come right out."
Joy was super excited about her new theory.

She went for a big bite of the shiny apple.
"**Ouch!**" shouted Joy.

"Girls, is everything okay out there?"
Shouted Mom from her bedroom.

"Yes, Mom, we're fine,
there is nothing to worry about,"
Joy quickly responded.

"Okay, follow me," ordered Joy.
They tiptoed past Mom's bedroom door.

"Joy, it's cool that you tried,
but maybe Mom is right.
You just have to be patient.
Get some sleep, and your tooth
will be out before you know it," I said.

Joy pulled the string from the pocket
of her white coat
with the look of a mad scientist in her eyes.
"Now, we're going to tie one end to my loose tooth
and the other end to my doorknob.
I'll stand still, you slam the door, and BOOM: tooth!"

"Are you absolutely sure about this?"
I asked Joy. Joy eagerly shook her head yes.

"Alright, remember I said you should listen to Mom,
but here goes nothing!"

BANG! The door slammed shut,
and Joy's body hit the floor.
She held her mouth and began to cry.

Mom rushed into the room,
"What in the world is going on here?"
Mom said in her sternest voice.

"I tried to make my tooth come out, and I hurt myself," mumbled Joy, with her hand still covering her mouth. Mom gave her the 'feel-better' hug.

"Honey, I'm so sorry you got hurt," said Mom.

"I think it's best for me to be patient,
and let my tooth fall out when it is ready," said Joy.

"I think that's a great idea.
You must have worked up an appetite now.
Let's eat," said Mom.

"Thank goodness! I almost died of starvation,"
I exclaimed.

Joy enjoyed her breakfast and exclaimed,
"Wh.. what?! You mean all I had to do was eat
a chocolate chip waffle? You've gotta be kidding me!"

"No, all you needed to do was be patient,"
I reminded her. We laughed and laughed...

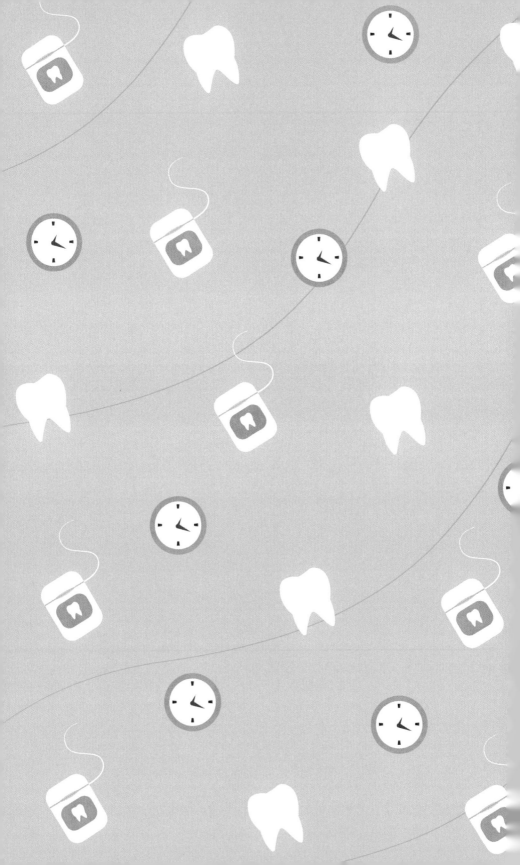

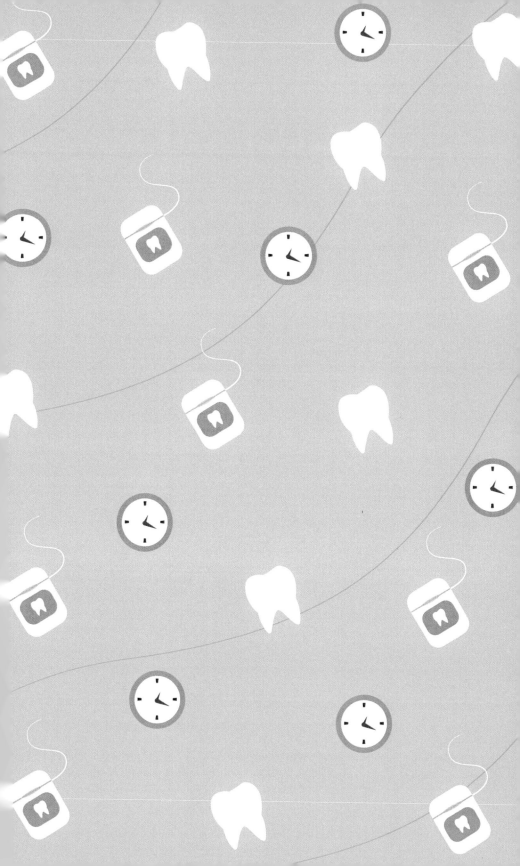

Made in the USA
Middletown, DE
17 June 2024

55787329R00020